Aunt Matilda
and Me
Go Into Town

Balboa Press books may be ordered through booksellers or by contacting:

Balboa Press
A Division of Hay House
1663 Liberty Drive
Bloomington, IN 47403
www.balboapress.com.au
1 (877) 407-4847

ISBN: 978-1-5043-2036-8 (sc)
ISBN: 978-1-5043-2035-1 (e)

Print information available on the last page.

Balboa Press rev. date: 01/16/2020

BALBOA.PRESS
A DIVISION OF HAY HOUSE

Aunt Matilda and Me Go Into Town

Dave Henry Pelham

Oh my Aunt Matilda had big googly eye's,
and a smile that embraced the day's early skies.

Aunt Matilda was funny with her big furry old hat,
that she wore every day - that scared even her big fat black cat...

Aunt Matilda wore fancy clothes with a big goofy smile,
and made no care of the fashion or style.

Today's town visit was a pink top here and green pants there,
this was perfect in her eye's - but other's would stare.

Aunt Matilda was carefree but still proud,
She made no nevermind in town with her head high in the crowd.

That big open smile with eye's she called grace,
But the clothes she wore were in everyone's face.

Blinded by colours and walking into a door - people would laugh,
but not Aunt Matilda, as she just flicked over
her yellow with orange dots scarf.

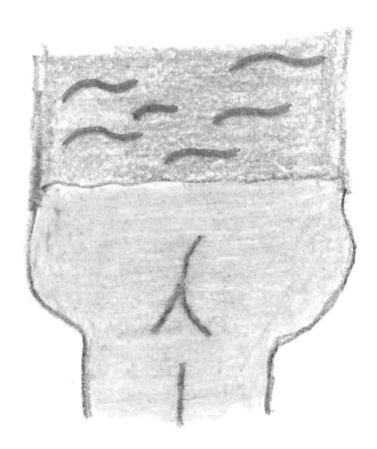

Walking with pride to her next shop - her big bottom naturally
seen, Aunt Matilda cared not - for today she is in green.

The colour of grass, plants and shop paintwork don't you know,
green was worn today to try to cover and blend in her big show..

Smiling at all and then - trip - as she walks, quickly
up and still walking as proud as she can,

I was behind watching those laughing - when
I should have been holding her hand.

Aunt Matilda brought lollies for me and a book for her to read,
She had brushed her trip off, but not me, as I
waited outside hiding my face in my sleeve.

As she walked out again more laughter is heard,
Those colours and hat and waiting for her to trip
again - seem to have struck a nerve.

Aunt Matilda just smiles, and walks on by,
telling me to catch up to her eye.

Her hand is out, no dought for me to hold. I am embarrassed and I'd rather not, but my Aunty is bold.

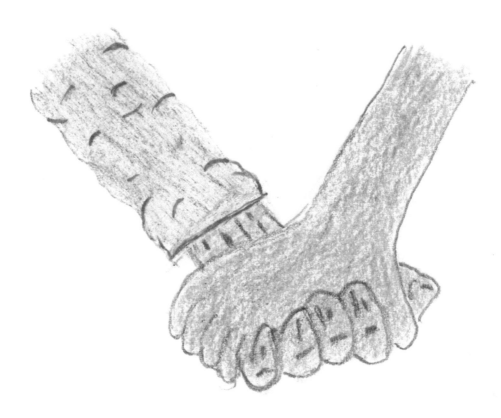

As she reaches for me, I take that hand - we walk
as they laugh - and I am feeling sad.

We sit for a bite at a cafe nearby,
I try to sit alone as she eats so fast, but Aunt Matilda then sadly sighs.

I ask what is wrong and she replies so sweet.
"I wanted a day with my Niece, with a little treat."

"I may be laughed at by people", as food swings from her lips,
"but that is fine with me, but I did hope to
not be shamed by my family"..

"I dress like this - as that is who I am,
And to help others and the wounded bird or animal - I do all I can".

This made me sniff a tear now too - as I seen a good heart,
people may laugh and joke at her two left feet and different dress art.

But my aunty has courage and wears colours so bright,
Maybe to shine so many can see right.....

My Aunt Matilda is so we may all see too.
Don't try to please others.. Just try being YOU..

THE END
BY **Dave Henry Pelham**

Next book: **Aunt Matilda and Me - Go to the beach**

What weird, crazy thing will my aunt say and do at the beach?
A great read for those who like to giggle and
laugh... Do you like to giggle and laugh?

Printed in the United States
By Bookmasters